THE IGUANA BROTHERS

A Tale of Two Lizards

Written by **TONY JOHNSTON** · Illustrated by **MARK TEAGUE**

SCHOLASTIC INC.

New York Toronto London Auckland Sydney

ISBN 0-590-47469-3

Text copyright © 1995 by Tony Johnston
Illustrations copyright © 1995 by Mark Teague
All rights reserved. Published by Scholastic Inc.

12 11 10 9 8 7 6 5 4 3 2 1   3   7 8 9/9 0 1 2/0

Printed in the United States of America   08

The illustrations in this book were painted with acrylics on
140-pound hot press watercolor paper.

Designed by Claire Counihan

For Tom Santana,
an iguana from Ecuador,
and
for Elise and Pat,
who keep him full
of bugs
—T.J.

For Brian and Devon
—M.T.

IT was a sunny morning in Mexico.
Tom and Dom were lolling on a roof.
A bug crawled near Dom. Dom's tongue
shot out.

Slurp. "Adiós, bug," said Dom.

A bug crawled near Tom. It crawled
on Tom. Tom did not move.

Dom moved. His tongue shot out.

Slurp. "Adiós, bug."

Dom slurped many bugs. Tom slurped none.

"Tom?" Dom asked at last. "I am catching
many bugs. You are catching none. Are you sick?"

"Sí, Dom. I am sick. I am sick of bugs."

"Ay, Tom," said Dom. "Ay-ay-ay. Bugs are
crunchy. Bugs are munchy. Bugs are deliciosos."

"Bugs are *gross-os*," said Tom. "You eat them all. They are not for me."

"But, Tom," said Dom. "Everybody eats bugs."

"You are wrong, Dom," said Tom. "People screech at bugs. They do not eat them. I will not eat them, either."

Dom said, "You will get thin, Tom. You will get *flaco, flaco, flaco*."

"I would rather be *flaco* than eat bugs."

"You will get pale, Tom," said Dom. "You will get *pálido, pálido, pálido*."

"Bugs make me pale already."

"And your tail will drop right off," said Dom.

Tom looked at his tail.
He asked, "*¿De veras?* Really?"
"*De veras*, Tom. Really."
"I will take that chance," said Tom.
Dom looked very worried.
"But what will you eat?" he asked.

Tom looked around. He saw a pig. The pig was big.

"I will eat pigs, Dom," he said.

Dom said, "Pigs are bigger than bugs. They will be hard to catch."

Tom thought about that. He blinked. He always blinked when he thought.

"You are right," Tom agreed. "I will not eat pigs."

Tom saw a snake.

"I will eat snakes, Dom," he said.

Then he cried, "SNAKES! No, no, no!
I am *loco*! Snakes are worse than bugs.
I will not eat snakes."

Tom blinked a lot. He thought a lot.
He saw something else. Flowers.

He said, "I will eat flowers, Dom.
Flowers are pretty."

"Flowers are prettier than pigs and snakes," said Dom. "But how do they taste?"

Tom tasted a flower.

He blinked. He thought.

He said, "Flowers taste pink, Dom. They taste better than bugs."

Dom tasted a flower.

He said, "*De veras*, Tom. Flowers taste better than bugs. You are my smartest brother."

"I am your *only* brother," Tom said.

"I know that." Dom grinned.

After that, Tom and Dom ate only flowers. No bugs. The flowers tasted good.

Tom and Dom were happy. Nobody got *flaco*. And nobody got *pálido*. And nobody's tail dropped off.

De veras.

It was a lazy afternoon. Dom was sunning himself on a vine.

Tom was not sunning. He was blinking. And thinking.

"Dom," he said. "I am thinking."

"*Por favor*, Tom," said Dom. "Think quietly. I am sunning."

"Stop sunning," said Tom. "Get up. I am thinking my best thought ever."

Dom opened one eye.

"The best, Tom? ¿*La mejor*?"
"*La mejor*, Dom. The best."
"Okay," said Dom.
"Tell me this best thought."
Tom said, "Dom, look
at me. What do you see?"
Dom looked at Tom
with one eye. He made
a wild guess.
"An iguana?" he asked.

"Wrong, Dom," said Tom. "You do not see an iguana." Dom was surprised. "What *do* I see, Tom?" "A dinosaur!" Dom opened his other eye. "That is your *best* thought, Tom?" "*Sí*. Isn't it truly amazing?" Dom said, "It is truly *loco*. You are not even sunning. And you have had too much sun."

"No, Dom," said Tom. "I *am* a dinosaur. You are, too."

Then Dom was truly amazed. He looked at himself carefully.

"I am, Tom?" he asked.

"*Claro que sí,* Dom."

"How can that be?"

Tom said, "Dinosaurs had scales, right?"

"Right," Dom agreed.

"And dinosaurs had long, lashy tails?"

"Right."

"And claws?"

"Right."

"And fearsome jaws?"

"Right."

Tom stopped. "Let me see your jaws, Dom," he said.

Dom showed his jaws.

"Are they fearsome, Tom?" he asked.

"Very fearsome."

Then Tom went on.

"Dinosaurs roared a lot," he said. "Let me hear you roar, Dom."

Dom made a little coughing sound. "*Rrrrr.*"

"Good, Dom," said Tom. "We have scales. We have tails. We have claws. And jaws. And we roar."

"We are dinosaurs!" the brothers cried.

"And, Dom," said Tom, "dinosaurs ruled the earth. Now you and I rule the earth."

Dom and Tom felt proud. They puffed themselves up. They strutted up and down the vine. They roared. *"Rrrrr."*

Along came a little lizard. It heard them roaring. It looked at them.

"YEK!" roared the little lizard.

"YEEEEEK!" screeched Tom and Dom. They nearly fell off the vine.

The little lizard laughed and ran away.

Tom said, "Dom, let's not be dinosaurs anymore."
"Let's not, Tom," said Dom. "Let's go sun ourselves."
Dom and Tom lay on a vine in the sun. Dom opened one eye.
"Tom?" he said.
"Sí, Dom?"
"I like being an iguana. I do not like ruling the earth."
"Me neither," said Tom.
"But, Tom?"
"Sí, Dom?"

"Can I rule something smaller?"
"What, Dom?"
"Can I rule this vine?"
"You can rule a leaf," said Tom.
"Fine."
They both laughed. Then they took
siestas in the sun.

It was evening now. The sun sank low. The stars began to glow. Tom and Dom were staring at the stars. Dom felt dreamy.

"Tom?" he said.

"Sí, Dom?"

"That is my favorite constellation."

"What is your favorite, Dom?" asked Tom.

"The Big Iguana."

"*Sí*. The Big Iguana is twinkly and beautiful," Tom agreed.

"I would like a friend just like that, Tom," said Dom dreamily. "Twinkly and beautiful."

Tom blinked. Tom thought.

He said, "*No hay problema*. I will find you one. A friend like the Big Iguana."

So Tom went looking for a friend for Dom.
He met a tarantula. It did not look like the
Big Iguana. But it was close enough.
"*Hola*, tarantula," said Tom. "Will you be
my brother's friend?"
"How many legs does he have?"
the tarantula asked.

Tom blinked. Tom thought.
"Four," he said at last.
"Four legs! How hilarious! He must
have eight legs to be *my* friend."
The tarantula crawled away, laughing.

Tom went on. He heard a *squawk*. He saw a toucan
in a tree. It did not look like the Big Iguana. But it was
colorful, even at night.

"*Hola*, toucan," said Tom. "I am looking for a friend
for my brother. Will you be his friend?"

"What color is he?" asked the toucan.

Tom blinked. Tom thought.

"He is the color of dirt," he said.

"How attractive," the toucan said.

"Can he fly?" it asked.

"No," said Tom.

"What a ninny," said the toucan.

"I cannot have a ninny for a friend."

The toucan flew off.

Tom went on. An armadillo came out of the bushes. It did not look like the Big Iguana. But Tom could not be fussy.

"*Hola*, armadillo," said Tom. "My brother needs a friend."

"Who doesn't?" said the armadillo. Then it asked, "What's so great about him?"

Tom blinked. Tom thought.

"Well, he eats flowers. He likes stars. And he rules a leaf."

"Rules a leaf?" asked the armadillo. "He sounds weird."

"My brother is not weird," Tom said.

"Can he roll into a ball like this?" the armadillo asked, rolling up tight.

Tom did not remember Dom rolling into a ball.

"No, he cannot do that," Tom said.

"Well, when he can roll into a ball, *maybe* I will be his friend," the armadillo said. And it rolled away.

Tom went home.

"Dom," he said sadly, "*lo siento*. I did not find
you a friend. Everyone I found was not right."

"Who did you find, Tom?"

"A tarantula. And a toucan. And an armadillo.
Not one single iguana."

"Oh," said Dom. Then he cried, "OH!"

"What?" asked Tom.

Dom said, "*You* are an iguana, Tom."

"*Es cierto,*" said Tom.

"And you are my brother," said Dom.

"*Sí.*"

"Can brothers be friends, Tom?"

Tom blinked. Tom thought. "*¡Claro que sí!*" he shouted.

"Brothers can be friends!" they both shouted.

Then Dom said, "I like you better than
the Big Iguana, Tom. He cannot eat flowers.
He cannot be a dinosaur. He can only twinkle."
Tom felt good. He felt like twinkling.
So did Dom.